Dangerous Rescue

Adapted by Brandon T. Snider
Based on the episode "Endangered Species"
written by Andrew Robinson

LITTLE, BROWN & COMPANY
LB kids

Little, Brown and Company

Hachette Book Group
1290 Avenue of the Americas, New York, NY 10104
Visit us at lb-kids.com

LB kids is an imprint of Little, Brown and Company.
The LB kids name and logo are trademarks of Hachette Book Group, Inc.

The publisher is not responsible for websites (or their content) that are not owned by the publisher.

First Edition: January 2016

Library of Congress Cataloging-in-Publication Data

Names: Snider, Brandon T.
Title: Dangerous rescue / by Brandon T. Snider.
Other titles: At head of title: Transformers rescue bots
Description: First edition. | New York : Little, Brown and Company, 2016.
Identifiers: LCCN 2015020559 | ISBN 9780316265461 (paperback)
Subjects: | BISAC: JUVENILE FICTION / Action & Adventure / General. |
  JUVENILE FICTION / Humorous Stories. | JUVENILE FICTION / Media Tie-In.
Classification: LCC PZ7.S6798 Tr 2016 | DDC [E]—dc23 LC record available at
http://lccn.loc.gov/2015020559

ISBN 978-0-316-26546-1

10 9 8 7 6 5 4 3 2 1

CW

Printed in the United States of America

Licensed By:

One beautiful spring day, Cody, Frankie, and Kade join their Rescue Bot friend Boulder for some bird-watching in the park.

Kade sighs. "Only Boulder could enjoy a pastime that even *humans* know is boring."

"I find the variety and beauty of Earth birds to be inspiring. Cybertron doesn't have anything like this," explains Boulder. He checks his bird-watcher book.

"That one is a woodpecker, and she has *babies*!" whispers Boulder. Cody and Frankie climb to a high branch so they can get a better look.

"Hey, kids! Climb down from there! It doesn't look safe," says Kade. Suddenly, the tree branch snaps, and Cody and Frankie start to tumble toward the baby birds.

"Power up and energize!" says Boulder, springing into action. He catches the kids in one hand and uses his laser to slice away the tree branch with the other.

"Are the baby birds okay?" asks Frankie. The tiny creatures hop onto Boulder's hand.

"They're wonderful," Boulder says, smiling. The mother bird hops onto Boulder's head and gently pecks him. "Hey, that tickles!"

Back at the firehouse, Doc Greene explains the meaning behind Boulder's discovery. "That's the first golden-crested woodpecker anyone has seen in forty years. We mustn't tell anyone about this. These birds need to be protected as an endangered species. The worst possible thing would be a crowd of tourists trampling through their habitat."

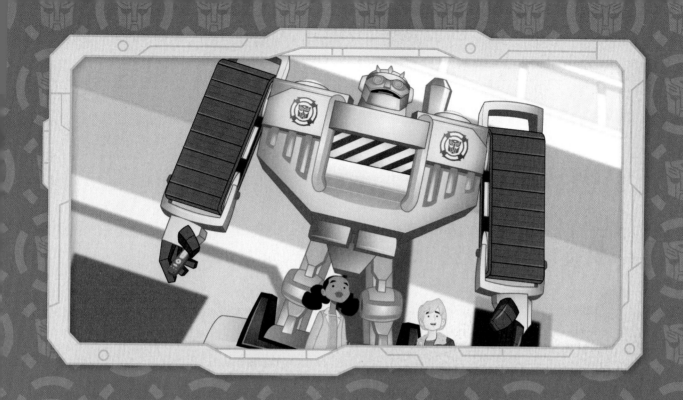

"What's an endangered species?" asks Boulder.

"An endangered species is an animal that's in danger of becoming extinct," answers Doc Greene. "If we can get those birds on the endangered species list, the government will step in to protect them."

Boulder loves protecting humans, but he thinks the birds should be kept safe, too.

Boulder talks with Chief Burns about the birds' safety. "Our mission is to serve and protect humans. But what about those creatures who need protection *from* humans?" he asks. "Those baby birds need guarding until Doc Greene can get them on the list."

But Chief Burns has concerns about the Rescue Bots protecting the birds full-time.

"I'll allow it on *one* condition: You can't neglect your *real* jobs," says the chief.

"Great!" exclaims Boulder, but not all the Rescue Bots want to be part of Boulder's mission.

"Our job is keeping people safe, not birds," grumbles Heatwave. "Count me out."

The next day, everyone else heads to Woodpecker's Grove to stand guard. Boulder suggests they clean up the area and plant some new flowers. He thinks the birds might like something pretty and fresh. The flowers attract a swarm of bees! Boulder has to plant the flowers a bit farther away.

Boulder thinks some nice, soothing music would calm the birds down after all the activity. He and Blades play some music, but it's too loud. The birds are even more frightened. Blades fumbles with the controls until he is able to lower the volume. Chief Burns stops by to see how things are going. He is surprised.

"I didn't realize your plan to protect the woodpeckers included scaring them," jokes Chief Burns.

Soon the babies come out of their hiding place. They look like they are ready to fly. Blades has some advice for the little birds. "Do what I did the first time. Just close your eyes and scream." Blades laughs.

Back near Town Hall, Mayor Luskey's car falls into a ditch. Heatwave and Kade rush to the rescue by themselves!

"We're carrying this whole load while everyone else is babysitting. Those birds don't look so endangered to me," says Kade.

"Did you say *endangered*?" asks Mayor Luskey.

Kade is in trouble now. No one is supposed to know about the birds.

"As mayor, I order you to come clean!" says Mayor Luskey.

"I, uh, *heard* there's a family of golden-crested woodpeckers that everyone thinks are extinct. But it's a secret. *Please* don't say anything," Kade pleads.

"Don't worry, my boy. I know how to keep a secret," says Mayor Luskey.

Heatwave changes into his vehicle mode. Kade hops in, and they drive away. Mayor Luskey smiles and waves as they depart.

Mayor Luskey makes a phone call. "Get out your floaties, because we're about to be swimming in tourists." He is up to something.

Later, the Rescue Bots and Cody watch as the mayor makes a big proclamation on the steps of Town Hall. "I'm thrilled to announce the rediscovery of the golden-crested woodpecker, right here in Griffin Rock!" says Mayor Luskey.

Cody can't believe what he is hearing. How did the mayor find out about the birds?

Cody gets a call later from reporter Huxley Prescott demanding to know who discovered the birds and where they are located. Boulder disguises his voice and handles the situation. He tells Huxley that the birds need to be left alone.

"That's the end of that," Boulder says, hanging up the phone. But he is wrong.

The next day, Huxley persuades Kade to disclose the location of the birds' nest. Then the mayor turns the spotlight on himself yet again. He announces where the woodpeckers are living.

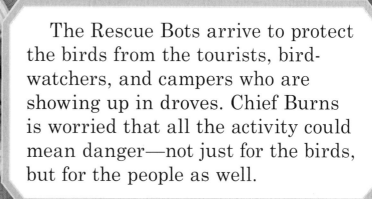

The Rescue Bots arrive to protect the birds from the tourists, bird-watchers, and campers who are showing up in droves. Chief Burns is worried that all the activity could mean danger—not just for the birds, but for the people as well.

Oh no! An out-of-control campfire causes sparks to fly into Woodpecker's Grove!

Quickly, the Rescue Bots roll into action and help the people get to safety. Blades uses his scoop claw to douse the fire from above.

When Heatwave arrives, he blasts the flames on the ground.

Boulder shovels dirt onto the fire. The Bots put the fire out!

The townsfolk are saved! But the birds flew away during the commotion. Luckily, Doc Greene tagged them so he could track their location.

"I am sure the birds will return to their home in no time," says Doc Greene.

"Perhaps there's a way the birds can be safe and a way for people to still see them?" wonders Cody. That gives Doc Greene an idea.

"After consulting with Doc Greene, I'm pleased to announce the opening of the Luskey Bird Sanctuary: a haven for endangered birds and the people who will pay to see them," says Mayor Luskey. Thankfully, Doc Greene has some points to add.

"We'll only admit a few people at a time so as not to disturb the birds. Our webcam will allow bird-watchers all over the world to enjoy our golden-crested friends as they rebuild their population," says Doc Greene.

A great compromise has been reached, and now everyone can enjoy the birds without troubling them.

"Yay us!" shouts Boulder as the baby woodpeckers take a seat on their hero's head.